F   Christopher, Matt
CHR

Johnny No Hit

$12.45 325470714847

AUG 11   DATE

JOHNNY NO HiT

JOHNNY NO HiT

MATT CHRISTOPHER

Illustrated by Ray Burns

Little, Brown and Company

Boston Toronto London

3254707148467

Library of Congress Cataloging in Publication Data

Christopher, Matthew F
  Johnny No Hit.

  SUMMARY: Threatened by a beating if he hits against Roy's pitching, Johnny almost loses a ballgame for his team.
  [1. Baseball — Fiction] I. Burns, Raymond.
II. Title.
PZ7.C458Jp   [Fic]   77-5488
ISBN 0-316-13974-2

BP

*Published simultaneously in Canada
by Little, Brown & Company (Canada) Limited*

PRINTED IN THE UNITED STATES OF AMERICA

10 9 8 7 6 5

To Michael

A familiar face peeked around
the corner of the dugout. It surprised
Johnny Webb as he stood in the on-
deck circle.

"Hi, Webby," Roy Burke greeted
him. A baseball cap rested on his mop
of red hair. "I want to see you after
the game. Okay?"

Johnny stared at him. He hated
that nickname. "Why?" he asked.
The last person he wanted to meet
anywhere was Roy Burke.

"You'll find out," said Roy, cracking
a wry grin. Then he was gone.

Johnny's heart pounded. *What
does Roy want to see me about?* he
thought. Two days ago Roy had almost run into him with a moped.

Whether he had done it on purpose,
just to scare him, Johnny didn't know.
Mo Jackson hit into a double play,
and Johnny stepped to the plate.

"Blast it, Johnny!" cried Coach Franks from the third-base coaching box.

"Make it a perfect day, Johnny!" said Bucky Raymond, the next batter. Johnny had two hits out of two times at bat so far.

He rubbed the handle of the bat,
noticing how sweaty his palms were
all of a sudden. The bases were clean.

Out in left field the scoreboard told
the story:

  Saddlebags 0 0 3 0 3
  Vikings   1 0 2 0 1

Ted Connors, pitching for the
Vikings, wound up. He pitched.
The ball breezed in, belt high. Johnny
didn't swing.

TEAM	1	2	3	4	5	6	7	8	9	TOTAL
SADDLEBAGS	0	0	3	0	3					
VIKINGS	1	0	2	0	1					

"Steerike!" boomed the ump.

Johnny knew he had missed a good pitch. *Why didn't I swing?* he thought.

He watched the next pitch come in, high and inside. This time he swung— and missed.

"Strike two!" yelled the ump.

Johnny stepped out of the box and rubbed the handle of the bat again. He was nervous. The image of Roy Burke's face was an ugly picture in his mind.

"Strike him out, Ted!" yelled a harsh voice. "That batter's just a big bluff!"

That was Roy's voice! Johnny thought.

Pressing his lips together hard, he
stepped back into the box. *Big bluff,
am I?* he said to himself.

Ted wound up, and delivered. The
pitch blazed in. Johnny swung. *Crack!*
It was a long blow to left field!

Johnny dropped his bat and ran to first base. Then to second. He stopped on third for a long triple!

"Nice smash, Johnny!" said Coach Franks. "That's three hits in a row, slugger."

Johnny felt good. *There, Roy!* he thought. *How do you like those apples?*

Bucky flied out. Three outs. The Saddlebags ran out to the field. Johnny got his glove and trotted to his short-stop position. It was the last half inning of the game.

Tony Mills mowed down the first batter. The next two grounded out to the infield. The game was over, the Saddlebags winning, 6 to 4.

Even though he was happy that his team had won, Johnny felt as tight as a banjo string. The thought of meeting Roy Burke worried him.

He headed out of the baseball park with Jimmy Krane and Les Moss, hoping that Roy had forgotten to wait for him. But just as they emerged from

the park, Johnny felt a hand tap him
on the shoulder. He turned and there
was Roy.

"Hi, Webby," said Roy.

Johnny froze.

"Don't be so nosy, you guys," said
Roy, as Jimmy and Les glanced at him.
"This is just between Webb and me."

The two boys continued on their way. Even *they* didn't want any trouble with Roy.

"What do you want, Roy?" Johnny asked, trying to act brave. Deep inside he felt like jelly.

"I'm pitching for Sugar Creek, and we're playing you Saddlebaggers next week," said Roy gruffly. "Everybody says you're a good hitter. Well, buddy—if you just touch my pitches you're going to get it from me. You get the point, Johnny Webb?"

Johnny, his face hot and sweaty,

looked into Roy's blazing eyes and nodded.

"Good," said Roy, the smile on his face widening. He turned and ran across the street to join a group of boys.

"What did he want?" Les asked as Johnny rejoined him and Jimmy.

"He just wanted to know how many hits I got," Johnny lied.

At home, Johnny changed his clothes and went on his newspaper route. *Maybe by next week—before the Saddlebags–Sugar Creek game—I might come down with a cold,* he thought. Anything could happen by then, he hoped.

Late the next afternoon, when
he went to the street corner to pick
up his papers, Roy Burke was already
there reading a copy.

"Hi, Webby," Roy greeted him
cheerfully. "Say, man, you did all
right yesterday. Two singles, a triple,
and five runs batted in. Not bad."

"Listen, Roy, the name is Johnny, not Webby, and you're not supposed to read my customers' papers," said Johnny. He started to pile the other newspapers into his bag. "Anyway, I've got to get going. I'm late already."

Roy fixed his eyes on him. "Look
again, *Webby*," he said. "You're talk-
ing to me. Roy. Now just cool it a
minute while I see what the Cincinnati
Reds did yesterday."

Johnny paled, and became impatient

as he waited for Roy to finish reading. He didn't dare say any more. He didn't want trouble from Roy.

At last Roy finished reading the article. He folded the paper and handed it to Johnny. "Thanks, Webby," he said. "My Reds won. And so will my Sugar Creek," he added, and rose to his feet. Chuckling, he ran off down the street.

On the day of the game, Johnny felt as healthy as could be. It was the first time in his life that he wished he weren't.

Sugar Creek had first bats, and right off they scored two runs.

The Saddlebags did nothing during
their turn at bat. Then Sugar Creek
picked up another run in the top of
the second, spreading their lead,
3 to 0.

Johnny, leading off in the bottom
half of the inning, met Roy's eyes
squarely as he faced the rugged

pitcher. Roy's threat rang in his mind
like a clanging bell. He felt as if he
were turned into a statue as two
pitches whizzed by him. Both were
strikes.

"Swing, Johnny!" yelled Eddie
Taylor, coaching at first.

The next pitch streaked in. Johnny
swung. *Whiff!*

"You're out!" cried the ump.

Johnny walked out of the box, his head down. No one except him knew that he had struck out on purpose. Struck out, because he was afraid of Roy.

Bucky, next to bat, flied out to center field. Then Les blasted out a double, and scored on Bill Hawley's single through the pitcher's box. Tony Mills drove in Bill with a colossal triple, but died on third as leadoff man Benny Farlan popped out to the infield.

Johnny avoided Roy's eyes as he ran out to his position. He felt sure he could hit Roy's pitches. But if he did—Johnny shuddered to think of what Roy might do to him. *He would probably break my arm so that I'd never be able to play ball again,* Johnny thought.

Sugar Creek scored two more runs in the top of the third. In the bottom

of the inning the Saddlebags picked
up one run.

Again Johnny came to bat, and
again he failed to hit.

I'm a coward, he confessed to himself.
*I shouldn't be playing, not if I'm going
to let Roy Burke keep me scared half to
death.*

Neither team scored in the fourth
inning. In the top of the fifth, Sugar
Creek got two men on, but neither one
of them could score. The Saddlebags
came to bat, trailing 5 to 3, and
looking down in the dumps.

"Come on, you guys!" cried Coach
Franks, trying to pep them up. "Look
alive, will you?"

31

Benny was up, and smashed
Roy's first pitch over second base for
a single. Jimmy belted a streaking shot
to left that was caught. Then Eddie
Taylor drew a walk. Two men on, one
out.

Johnny, on deck, watched Roy pitch four straight balls to Mo Jackson.

The rat, thought Johnny. *He walked Mo on purpose so that he could pitch to me. He thinks I'm going to strike out again.*

Roy smiled as Johnny stepped to the plate.

"Strike!" yelled the ump as Roy's
first pitch cut the inside corner.

Sweat began to pour down Johnny's
face.

Roy stretched, and pitched again.
The ball streaked in. It looked good.
But Johnny didn't swing.

"Strike two!" boomed the ump.

Johnny saw the smirk on Roy's face. *One more strike and I'm out,* Johnny thought bitterly.

Suddenly he thought of something else. Something that Roy Burke, himself, had yelled to him in the game against the Vikings.

A hard look came over Johnny's face. "Okay, Roy!" he shouted. "Come on! Pitch!"

Roy stared at him. He stretched,
then fired the ball. Like a white bul-
let, it blazed in. Johnny swung.

Crack! The ball shot like a missile toward left field! It climbed higher and higher, then disappeared over the fence! A home run!

A thunder of applause exploded
from the fans as Johnny circled the
bases behind the other three runners.
At home plate he was greeted by the
members of his team, all anxious to
shake his hand.

When the game was finally over,
the Saddlebags won it, 7 to 5.

Johnny met Roy near the park gate.
Roy's face turned red as he looked
at Johnny.

"You called me a big bluff, Roy,"
said Johnny. "Who's a big bluff now?"

Roy glanced at Johnny but said
nothing as he walked out of the park.

Johnny whistled happily as he
joined his friends for the walk home.

Books by Matt Christopher

Sports Stories

THE LUCKY BASEBALL BAT
BASEBALL PALS
BASKETBALL SPARKPLUG
TWO STRIKES ON JOHNNY
LITTLE LEFTY
TOUCHDOWN FOR TOMMY
LONG STRETCH AT FIRST BASE
BREAK FOR THE BASKET
CRACKERJACK HALFBACK
BASEBALL FLYHAWK
SINK IT, RUSTY
CATCHER WITH A GLASS ARM
TOO HOT TO HANDLE
THE COUNTERFEIT TACKLE
LONG SHOT FOR PAUL
THE TEAM THAT COULDN'T LOSE
THE YEAR MOM WON THE PENNANT
THE BASKET COUNTS
CATCH THAT PASS!
SHORTSTOP FROM TOKYO
LUCKY SEVEN
JOHNNY LONG LEGS
LOOK WHO'S PLAYING FIRST BASE
TOUGH TO TACKLE
THE KID WHO ONLY HIT HOMERS
FACE-OFF
MYSTERY COACH
ICE MAGIC
NO ARM IN LEFT FIELD
JINX GLOVE
FRONT COURT HEX
THE TEAM THAT STOPPED MOVING
GLUE FINGERS
THE PIGEON WITH THE TENNIS ELBOW
THE SUBMARINE PITCH
POWER PLAY
FOOTBALL FUGITIVE
THE DIAMOND CHAMPS
JOHNNY NO HIT

Animal Stories

DESPERATE SEARCH
STRANDED
EARTHQUAKE
DEVIL PONY